WILBUR'S ADVENTURE

For Gordon
—M.K.

Wilbur's Adventure
Text copyright 1952 by E. B. White,
text copyright © renewed 1980 by E. B. White
Text from *Charlotte's Web*, by E. B. White
Illustrations copyright © 2008 by Maggie Kneen
Manufactured in China. All rights reserved.
No part of this book may be used or reproduced in any
manner whatsoever without written permission except in the case of
brief quotations embodied in critical articles and reviews. For information
address HarperCollins Children's Books, a division of HarperCollins
Publishers, 1350 Avenue of the Americas, New York, NY 10019.
www.harpercollinschildrens.com
Library of Congress Cataloging-in-Publication Data
White, E. B. (Elwyn Brooks), 1899–1985. Wilbur's adventure : a Charlotte's web picture book / by E. B.
White ; illustrated by Maggie Kneen. — 1st ed. p. cm. Summary: Relates the experiences of Wilbur the pig
when a goose hears that he is bored and encourages him to experience freedom outside his fence. ISBN-
10: 0-06-078164-5 (trade bdg.) — ISBN-13: 978-0-06-078164-4 (trade bdg.) ISBN-10: 0-06-078165-3 (lib.
bdg.) — ISBN-13: 978-0-06-078165-1 (lib. bdg.) [1. Pigs—Fiction. 2. Farm life—Fiction.] I. Kneen,
Maggie, ill. II. Title. PZ7.W58277Wil 2008 2006021466 [E]—dc22

Design by Stephanie Bart-Horvath
1 2 3 4 5 6 7 8 9 10 ❖ First Edition

WILBUR'S ADVENTURE

A *CHARLOTTE'S WEB* PICTURE BOOK

BY E. B. White

ILLUSTRATED BY Maggie Kneen

HarperCollins*Publishers*

*T*HE BARN WAS VERY LARGE. It was very old. It smelled of hay and it smelled of manure. It smelled of the perspiration of tired horses and the wonderful sweet breath of patient cows. It often had a sort of peaceful smell—as though nothing bad could happen ever again in the world. It smelled of grain and of harness dressing and of axle grease and of rubber boots and of new rope. And whenever the cat was given a fish-head to eat, the barn would smell of fish. But mostly it smelled of hay, for there was always hay in the great loft up overhead. And there was always hay being pitched down to the cows and the horses and the sheep.

The barn was pleasantly warm in winter when the animals spent most of their time indoors, and it was pleasantly cool in summer when the big doors stood wide open to the breeze. The barn had stalls on the main floor for the work horses, tie-ups on the main floor for the cows, a sheepfold down below for the sheep, a pigpen down below for Wilbur, and it was full of all sorts of things that you find in barns: ladders, grindstones, pitch forks, monkey wrenches, scythes, lawn mowers, snow shovels, ax handles, milk pails, water buckets, empty grain sacks, and rusty rat traps. It was the kind of barn that swallows like to build their nests in. It was the kind of barn that children like to play in. And the whole thing was owned by Fern's uncle, Mr. Homer L. Zuckerman.

Wilbur's new home was in the lower part of the barn, directly underneath the cows. Mr. Zuckerman knew that a manure pile is a good place to keep a young pig. Pigs need warmth, and it was warm and comfortable down there in the barn cellar on the south side.

Fern came almost every day to visit him. She found an old milking stool that had been discarded, and she placed the stool in the sheepfold next to Wilbur's pen. Here she sat quietly during the long afternoons, thinking and listening and watching Wilbur. The sheep soon got to know her and trust her. So did the geese, who lived with the sheep. All the animals trusted her, she was so quiet and friendly. Mr. Zuckerman did not allow her to take Wilbur out, and he did not allow her to get into the pigpen. But he told Fern that she could sit on the stool and watch Wilbur as long as she wanted to.

It made her happy just to be near the pig, and it made Wilbur happy to know that she was sitting there, right outside his pen. But he never had any fun—no walks, no rides, no swims.

One afternoon in June, when Wilbur was almost two months old, he wandered out into his small yard outside the barn. Fern had not arrived for her usual visit. Wilbur stood in the sun feeling lonely and bored.

"There's never anything to do around here," he thought. He walked slowly to his food trough and sniffed to see if anything had been overlooked at lunch. He found a small strip of potato skin and ate it.

His back itched, so he leaned against the fence and rubbed against the boards. When he tired of this, he walked indoors, climbed to the top of the manure pile, and sat down. He didn't feel like going to sleep, he didn't feel like digging, he was tired of standing still, tired of lying down. "I'm less than two months old and I'm tired of living," he said. He walked out to the yard again.

"When I'm out here," he said, "there's no place to go but in. When I'm indoors, there's no place to go but out in the yard."

"That's where you're wrong, my friend, my friend," said a voice.

Wilbur looked through the fence and saw the goose standing there.

"You don't have to stay in that dirty-little dirty-little dirty-little yard," said the goose, who talked rather fast. "One of the boards is loose. Push on it, push-push-push on it, and come on out!"

"What?" said Wilbur. "Say it slower!"

"At-at-at, at the risk of repeating myself," said the goose, "I suggest that you come on out. It's wonderful out here."

"Did you say a board was loose?"

"That I did, that I did," said the goose.

Wilbur walked up to the fence and saw that the goose was right—one board was loose. He put his head down, shut his eyes, and pushed. The board gave way. In a minute he had squeezed through the fence and was standing in the long grass outside his yard. The goose chuckled.

"How does it feel to be free?" she asked.

"I like it," said Wilbur. "That is, I *guess* I like it." Actually, Wilbur felt queer to be outside his fence, with nothing between him and the big world.

"Where do you think I'd better go?"

"Anywhere you like, anywhere you like," said the goose. "Go down through the orchard, root up the sod! Go down through the garden, dig up the radishes! Root up everything! Eat grass! Look for corn! Look for oats! Run all over! Skip and dance, jump and prance! Go down through the orchard and stroll in the woods! The world is a wonderful place when you're young."

"I can see that," replied Wilbur. He gave a jump in the air, twirled, ran a few steps, stopped, looked all around, sniffed the smells of afternoon, and then set off walking down through the orchard. Pausing in the shade of an apple tree, he put his strong snout into the ground and began pushing, digging, and rooting. He felt very happy. He had plowed up quite a piece of ground before anyone noticed him.

Mrs. Zuckerman was the first to see him. She saw him from the kitchen window, and she immediately shouted for the men.

"Ho-*mer*!" she cried. "Pig's out! Lurvy! Pig's out! Homer! Lurvy! Pig's out. He's down there under that apple tree."

"Now the trouble starts," thought Wilbur. "Now I'll catch it."

The goose heard the racket and she, too, started hollering. "Run-run-run downhill, make for the woods, the woods!" she shouted to Wilbur. "They'll never-never-never catch you in the woods."

The cocker spaniel heard the commotion and he ran out from the barn to join the chase. Mr. Zuckerman heard, and he came out of the machine shed where he was mending a tool. Lurvy, the hired man, heard the noise and came up from the asparagus patch where

he was pulling weeds. Everybody walked toward Wilbur and Wilbur didn't know what to do. The woods seemed a long way off, and anyway, he had never been down there in the woods and wasn't sure he would like it.

"Get around behind him, Lurvy," said Mr. Zuckerman, "and drive him toward the barn! And take it easy—don't rush him! I'll go and get a bucket of slops."

The news of Wilbur's escape spread rapidly among the animals on the place. Whenever any creature broke loose on Zuckerman's farm, the event was of great interest to the others. The goose shouted to the nearest cow that Wilbur was free, and soon all the cows knew. Then one of the cows told one of the sheep, and soon all the sheep knew.

The lambs learned about it from their mothers. The horses, in their stalls in the barn, pricked up their ears when they heard the goose hollering; and soon the horses caught on to what was happening. "Wilbur's out," they said. Every animal stirred and lifted its head and became excited to know that one of his friends had got free and was no longer penned up or tied fast.

Wilbur didn't know what to do or which way to run. It seemed as though everybody was after him. "If this is what it's like to be free," he thought, "I believe I'd rather be penned up in my own yard."

The cocker spaniel was sneaking up on him from one side,

Lurvy the hired man was sneaking up on him from the other side. Mrs. Zuckerman stood ready to head him off if he started for the garden, and now Mr. Zuckerman was coming down toward him carrying a pail. "This is really awful," thought Wilbur. "Why doesn't Fern come?" He began to cry.

The goose took command and began to give orders.

"Don't just stand there, Wilbur! Dodge about, dodge about!" cried the goose. "Skip around, run toward me, slip in and out, in and out, in and out! Make for the woods! Twist and turn!"

The cocker spaniel sprang for Wilbur's hind leg. Wilbur jumped and ran. Lurvy reached out and grabbed. Mrs. Zuckerman screamed at Lurvy. The goose cheered for Wilbur. Wilbur dodged between Lurvy's legs. Lurvy missed Wilbur and grabbed the spaniel instead. "Nicely done, nicely done!" cried the goose. "Try it again, try it again!"

"Run downhill!" suggested the cows.

"Run toward me!" yelled the gander.

"Run uphill!" cried the sheep.

"Turn and twist!" honked the goose.

"Jump and dance!" said the rooster.

"Look out for Lurvy!" called the cows.

"Look out for Zuckerman!" yelled the gander.

"Watch out for the dog!" cried the sheep.

"Listen to me, listen to me!" screamed the goose.

Poor Wilbur was dazed and frightened by this hullabaloo. He didn't like being the center of all this fuss. He tried to follow the instructions his friends were giving him, but he couldn't run downhill and uphill at the same time, and he couldn't turn and twist when he was jumping and dancing, and he was crying so hard he could barely see anything that was happening. After all, Wilbur was a very young pig—not much more than a baby, really. He wished Fern were there to take him in her arms and comfort him. When he looked up and saw Mr. Zuckerman standing quite close to him, holding a pail of warm slops, he felt relieved. He lifted his nose and sniffed. The smell was delicious— warm milk, potato skins, wheat middlings, Kellogg's Corn Flakes, and a popover left from the Zuckermans' breakfast.

"Come, pig!" said Mr. Zuckerman, tapping the pail. "Come pig!" Wilbur took a step toward the pail.

"No-no-no!" said the goose. "It's the old pail trick, Wilbur. Don't fall for it, don't fall for it! He's trying to lure you back into captivity-ivity. He's appealing to your stomach."

Wilbur didn't care. The food smelled appetizing. He took another step toward the pail.

"Pig, pig!" said Mr. Zuckerman in a kind voice, and began walking slowly toward the barnyard, looking all about him innocently, as if he didn't know that a little white pig was following along behind him.

"You'll be sorry-sorry-sorry," called the goose.

Wilbur didn't care. He kept walking toward the pail of slops.

"You'll miss your freedom," honked the goose. "An hour of freedom is worth a barrel of slops."

Wilbur didn't care.

When Mr. Zuckerman reached the pigpen, he climbed over the fence and poured the slops into the trough. Then he pulled the loose board away from the fence, so that there was a wide hole for Wilbur to walk through.

"Reconsider, reconsider!" cried the goose.

Wilbur paid no attention. He stepped through the fence into his yard. He walked to the trough and took a long drink of slops, sucking in the milk hungrily and chewing the popover. It was good to be home again.

While Wilbur ate, Lurvy fetched a hammer and some 8-penny nails and nailed the board in place. Then he and Mr. Zuckerman leaned lazily on the fence and Mr. Zuckerman scratched Wilbur's back with a stick.

"He's quite a pig," said Lurvy.

"Yes, he'll make a good pig," said Mr. Zuckerman.

Wilbur heard the words of praise. He felt the warm milk inside his stomach. He felt the pleasant rubbing of the stick along his itchy back. He felt peaceful and happy and sleepy. This had been a tiring afternoon. It was still only about four o'clock but Wilbur was ready for bed.

"I'm really too young to go out into the world alone," he thought as he lay down.